ROSWELL
FIRST CONTACT

TONY B. RICHARD

ROSWELL
FIRST CONTACT

EARTH'S SECRET ALLIANCE
MALCOLM DOW: EPISODE 1

TONY B. RICHARD

TIGERPETAL PRESS

Second Edition, April 2022

3 5 7 9 11 10 8 6 4 2

Cover designed by Perky Visuals
Interior designed & edited by Carolin Petersen
Typeset in Arno Pro & Kallisto

ISBN 978-1-7778185-7-9 (paperback, regular)
ISBN 978-1-7778185-9-3 (paperback, dyslexia font)
ISBN 978-1-7778185-8-6 (paperback, large print)
ISBN 978-1-7778185-4-8 (ebook)

Published by Tigerpetal Press
Chilliwack, BC, Canada
www.tigerpetalpress.ca

visit *www.tonybrichard.com*

Dedicated to my wife, Lydia, who has stood by my side through thick and thin. This book would not be possible without her.

Also dedicated to all people with dyslexia, those who persevere in the face of bullying, and those who are different in any way. Know that you are loved.

TABLE OF CONTENTS

PROLOGUE

"Status report?"

"Approaching the earth's atmosphere now, Captain."

The captain nodded, turning his eyes back to the screen. He slid his long blue fingers forward across the panel in front of him, then looked over at the engineer. "Keep it steady," he ordered. "I'm bringing it down."

The engineer nodded and swiveled her chair to the far side of her desk. Her fingers moved with ease across the touchscreen. "Ready, Captain."

"Perfect."

The spacecraft dipped, barely nudging the invisible ozone layer around the vibrant blue and green planet below. All seemed to be going as planned. Until it didn't.

Suddenly, alarms wailed. Red lights flashed. The captain's body seized. "Computer, give me virtual controls." He held his palms out flat and his shirt sleeves extended over his hands like gloves. Bringing his hands up, the captain began maneuvering the ship with precise twitches of his fingers. The turbulence rumbled through him. Clear glasses appeared over his eyes, and he pulled up the ship's status. Numbers flew across his vision. He gasped, and his skin flashed white like the depths of a dying star.

"The ship's losing power!" the engineer called from her desk. "The engine is down!" She ran her fingers over the illuminated metal. "Thrusters are losing power as well! Deflectors are down."

"And the hull?" the captain asked.

"The hull is holding, sir," she replied. "Should we deploy the parachute?"

"Not yet." The captain kept his hands steady. He was waiting for his moment. The limited thrusters stuttered and choked on their last few breaths of life, sending the ship shaking and trembling, but he held firm. "Not yet…"

The spacecraft blazed as it fell. Flames licked up around the sides, and clouds of smoke formed its tail.

"Now?"

"Not yet!"

The third passenger's trembling fingers gripped the edges of his seat. He gulped. "Captain, I think it would be wise to deploy the parachute now."

"The ship is still blazing. The parachute will fail. It will crash."

"It will crash anyway," the engineer pointed out. She shook her head. "Deploying parachute in three, two…"

The captain brought his hands back sharply and spread his fingers. "Now!" he cried.

The parachute deployed, and the ship lurched. Its speed cut in half, the fires died slightly, and it drifted down. They let out sighs of relief.

"Is it safe?" With the gloves and glasses gone, the captain inspected the monitor in front of him. Every readout was bright green. All except one. "What is wrong with this?" he asked, pointing to the screen. Another alarm blared, and the parachute ripped. The spacecraft dropped like a stone, and the earth rushed up to meet it.

CHAPTER ONE

JUST ANOTHER DAY

ROSWELL, NEW MEXICO
July 8, 1947

Private Malcolm Dow planted his feet firmly so he wouldn't bounce all over in the back of the transport truck. He didn't need to give the other soldiers any more reason to laugh. There were seven of them, talking and trading jokes. They acted like Malcolm wasn't even there. He felt a knot in his stomach.

Malcolm was second-generation army, but given how he was treated by his peers, he often didn't feel like it. Malcolm's thoughts drifted to his fathers—both of them. His birth dad, Jacob Dow, was a soldier who gave his life years ago to save Lieutenant Gerry Smith. Gerry was a friend of his father, and after his life had been saved, he felt the only way to repay his debt was to take care of Jacob's family. That was how Malcolm found himself, his mother, and his sister living with the Smiths—

Malcolm felt a kick. "Ow!" He looked up at Corporal Lawless, who was seated directly across from him.

"I don't know how you cheated during target practice today, but I'll find out!" Lawless growled. "Everyone knows blacks can't shoot." He was nearly in Malcolm's face, and his breath smelled foul.

Malcolm chuckled. Not the brightest guy. *I mean, how do you cheat at target practice? Besides, the color of your skin doesn't affect how well you shoot.* He didn't take the abuse personally. His mother always taught him to treat others the way he wanted to be treated, to show kindness in the face of hate. *"You can't always change other people's minds, son. Remember that. You can't control how they treat you, only how to treat them in return. Fight when you must, but when you don't have to, show love."* Malcolm vowed he would always show love.

Lawless was a man of bulky muscle; his blond hair was cropped close to his skull, and his skin was slightly red with sunburn. He often thought of himself as the best and never let others forget it. He treated everyone who was different from him just as poorly, and his lackeys were no better.

Malcolm glanced over at the other soldiers. They'd stopped talking and were all looking at him. Half of them were glaring like Lawless was, like lions ready to pounce. The other half just broke eye contact and went back to their conversations.

Lawless snarled. He grabbed hold of Malcolm's uniform collar and pulled. "I'm talking to you, Dow! Are you listening to me? I know you cheated! You just wait until we're alone—I'll beat it out of you."

Malcolm easily extracted himself from Lawless's grip. He sat back against the truck wall, fingers wrapped tightly around Lawless's hand as he said, "You tried that last week. How many bruises did you get?" Malcolm's lips curled into a hint of a smile, and he gave a sharp squeeze before letting go. He knew Lawless wouldn't admit that a black man could beat him in a fight, so he'd never report it as an assault, even if Malcolm was his subordinate. Especially since Malcolm was a private, it would be very embarrassing.

Some of the soldiers chuckled. Lawless turned pale, and his glare shifted rapidly between them and Malcolm. When

Lawless regained his composure, he gave them the evil eye. "What're you laughing at?" he said, leaning back again.

The others shared glances and snickered.

Lawless looked at Malcolm then back at the others. "Hey, what do you think crashed this time? A spy plane? A weather balloon?"

There were hums of agreement for each guess.

Malcolm figured Lawless was trying to change the topic, and it worked. Malcolm kept his mouth shut. He formed a few guesses of his own—even jokingly wondered if they'd find an alien ship, like in the comics he used to read, but wisely avoided inserting himself into their discussion.

CRASH SITE

The truck finally stopped a half hour later. Malcolm, being closest to the back, jumped out first. He looked around. In the distance was a rancher-style house, a barn, and a herd of cows among tumbleweeds and broken fences—presumably broken from last night's heavy winds. Other than that, there was nothing as far as the eye could see.

Where is the crash?

"This way, men!" Sergeant Highton called from the other side of one of the other large green trucks.

As Malcolm joined the others, they were all staring at something off in the distance. He followed their eyes. That was when he saw it. A massive disk-shaped silver object, he estimated about fifty feet across, right in front of him. With the bump on top, it kind of reminded him of an upside-down plate or a teacup saucer. It was already half-covered in sand from the winds earlier that morning, but from what he could see, the exterior was made of tin foil. It was ripped, and there were foil fragments all over the ground.

The lieutenant came around from the transport cab, and Highton yelled, "Attention!" Everyone stood up straight.

The lieutenant had his hands on his hips as he scanned the soldiers with cold brown eyes that could cut glass. "At ease. This may look unusual, but I'm told it's hollow, some kind of parachute. You know the drill! Make sure you get every bit of this foil, even way up by the hills. Dismissed!" He and Highton then walked to where the ranch owner, his son, and the local sheriff were standing. They kept looking over their shoulders at the large object, shaking their heads as they increased their paces.

The troops approached the object cautiously, looking in through the rips to see that it was indeed hollow. It was a parachute of some sort, although with the supports, Malcolm thought an umbrella would be a better word for it. He peered in as well.

In the center was a small bell-shaped object.

"Who's going to go in there and see what that thing is?" Lawless challenged. Clearly, he wasn't going to do it himself.

Everyone was silent. A few mumbles broke out, and eyes shifted back and forth. Malcolm looked over at the sergeant and lieutenant, who were in a deep discussion with the sheriff.

"Dow!" Lawless pointed at him. "Take point!" A wave of agreement rose from the others, and they all backed away, leaving Malcolm closest to the unknown object.

Malcolm had mixed emotions. *On one hand, it is an unlikely honor. On the other hand, he is putting me in potential danger. But I'm really curious what's under there. Could it be from outer space?* He took a deep breath and slowly ducked through a larger hole in the outer foil frame toward the center object. Half the other soldiers followed at a respectable distance behind, guns at the ready. Lawless and the other half spread out and took aim through different holes.

He peered at it from a distance, looking for any hazard warnings or identifying marks, but all he found were lines upon lines of jagged symbols that he didn't recognize. He leaned closer, squinting through the dark window. The glass must've been scorched in the landing because it was gritty and smudged, but he could still make out the faint outline of arms and legs.

Malcolm jerked away. *What?* He gasped.

"I think there's someone in there!" he shouted to the others, who were still watching him with guns at the ready. "And they're not moving!" Malcolm's heart was racing. The others might have been speaking, but Malcolm couldn't hear them over the sound of his own blood rushing through his ears. "They might be out of air!"

No one moved.

Malcolm grabbed the door handle and yanked hard, but it didn't budge. "Help me!"

As he desperately pulled the door, he looked up at the other soldiers. Wide-eyed and fidgeting, they made no move to help. Lawless and the others stayed frozen in place, guns aimed at the ship. Malcolm felt more confused and panicked than angry. *Why won't they help? Did they see something?* he wondered. *I hope that they don't accidentally pull the trigger.*

Malcolm looked around for something to use as a lever. He saw a dangling parachute support beam and pulled it down, then wedged the edge of it under the handle. He pushed hard. A moment later the door shifted, and there was a hissing noise, like air leaking out of a tire. Sand flew toward the door, and he realized the air was being sucked in, not blown out. Then the pressure released, and the door swung open, smacking Malcolm in the face. He fell to the ground.

"Ow," he mumbled, rubbing his nose. He looked up, squinting, but sand and dust filled his vision, sending him into a coughing fit. After the dust cleared, he cautiously stepped toward the vessel and looked inside. Three small people were strapped into the seats. Their hairless, bulging heads hung forward limply.

Are those…children? he wondered, even as his stomach churned at the thought. *Who would smuggle children?*

Malcolm stared for several seconds, and it was then that he began to really notice how odd the children looked. Their heads weren't just swollen, they were far bigger than they should be—their bodies were tiny in comparison—and they were an odd shade of gray.

He felt a lump in his throat. *They're not human!*

A jolt of adrenalin made his heart leap, and he jumped back, dropped the beam, and slammed the door shut while yelling, "Lieutenant!"

It took a minute for the lieutenant to appear outside, looking in through one of the larger rips in the parachute. "What? What's wrong?" He slowly worked his way past the frame.

Malcolm was shaking all over and trying to talk, but his tongue felt too large for his mouth. The words wouldn't form. Finally, he stuttered, "A-aliens!"

The lieutenant sneered, disbelieving. "Yeah, right!" He opened the door of the ship. "If this is some kind of joke, Dow, you're in for a lot of trouble." He turned, looked, then slammed the door shut. His face had turned the color of sour milk, and his mouth was moving just slightly, letting loose a string of curses.

Outside, the others were hovering, curious eyes on Malcolm and the lieutenant. Some that were close to him, were whispering to each other. Malcolm was sure that they had either seen what was inside or had heard what he had told the lieutenant.

The lieutenant blinked, collected himself, then turned around and yelled at them, "What are you all standing around for? I told you to clean up!" Then he pointed sharply at the vessel. "This container is off-limits! No one touch it, no one open it, no one even look at it! Do you hear me? No one!" With that, he rushed to the transport truck to use the radio.

Malcolm's heart raced a mile a minute. He felt dizzy, and a chill ran up and down his spine even though he was sweating. As he turned, he saw the other soldiers' pale faces and raised eyebrows. He wondered if they'd heard him shout. They started whispering to each other as they got back to work, sending curious, frightened glances in the vessel's direction.

Well, at least they are not looking at me, he thought, rubbing his hands together to stop them from trembling. *What am I supposed to do now?* A whole range of thoughts and emotions cycled through his mind. He was surprised that he felt sorry for the alien children rather than feeling scared. *What a horrific way to die.*

Wanting to be alone, he saw some foil fragments in the distance, picked up a collection bag, and headed in that direction, out of sight of the others.

I wonder if they were running from someone. Though the parachute was huge, the vessel was small; it could've been a lifeboat. Were they being hunted? Ostracized? Was it because they were different? A sudden heaviness weighed him down like someone had dropped a nuclear warhead into his ribcage.

CHAPTER TWO

STRANGER FROM ANOTHER WORLD

ROSWELL CRASH SITE, NEW MEXICO
July 8, 1947

Malcolm wandered around the desert, picking up debris and putting the pieces in his burlap sack. The image of the alien children haunted him. He could feel tears welling up and didn't know exactly why.

Toughen up, he told himself. *Men aren't supposed to cry!* He needed to be strong and stay strong, and that meant accepting his emotions and letting them pass. He let the lump form in his throat, but not a single tear fell from his eyes.

After about an hour, Malcolm felt drained. He'd just walked a mile in the hot desert sun after what was already shaping up to be a long day. Only then, when no one was around, did he allow the tears to fall. He crouched, stooping over as his breaths came in choked gasps, and his shoulders twitched and trembled.

Then he froze. The stubble of hairs along the nape of his neck stood on end—someone was watching him. It was just a hunch, but like all his hunches, he was certain. He could feel it. Malcolm took a deep breath and rubbed his eyes. He stood up and scanned the area, looking for other soldiers, but didn't see anyone. The only tracks in the sand were his own.

His mind shot back to the alien vessel. *I wonder if some aliens survived the crash. They could be watching me. But why?*

Back when he was ten, one of the radio dramas was about aliens who attacked the world. Was this an act of aggression? Probably not. But he couldn't unthink it.

His heart pounded, and his skin felt clammy. Then, his soldier instincts kicked in, and he dropped into a fighting stance. He leaned forward with fists raised, knees bent, and muscles tensed. Squinting his eyes against the sun, he turned in a full circle, scanning the desert for hostiles. His wrists rotated slowly. Still nothing but sand and tumbleweeds.

Is it nothing? Am I just overreacting? he thought. His searching gaze continued, two sides of him at war. His gut was telling him not to worry, but how could he be sure?

Malcolm had hunches like this before. They never made any sense, and there was nothing to validate them, but when he followed them, good things typically happened. He decided to trust his gut yet again, so he relaxed, grabbed his sack, and resumed picking up debris. "I know what it's like when people don't like you 'cause you look different," he said loudly as he continued to look for fragments of foil. The bodies he found were all gray. *Do they have different races on their planet?* "If you haven't noticed, I have black skin, and the other people here have white skin."

He didn't know if his hunches were correct or he was just talking to himself, but if whoever was watching him was scared, he'd need to give them a reason to come out. If not, it wasn't like anyone was out there to hear him anyway.

Something appeared out of the corner of his eye, and he looked up. A strange-looking man, about ten feet away, watching him. Malcolm glanced around but didn't see anything or anyone else. *Where did he come from?* Malcolm looked at the man and noticed that he was just a little shorter than himself. He was bald, had light purple skin and was wearing clothing that looked like the foil Malcolm had just been collecting.

He couldn't be human, but he wasn't gray like the children's bodies. *Why is he like the others but somehow different?* Malcolm wondered if he was a different kind of alien.

The alien broke the silence. "How did you know I was here?"

"I just had a hunch." Malcolm was surprised at how quickly and naturally he answered the strange 'man.'

"You are not scared? Like the others?"

Malcolm tensed, then looked away as he thought about Lawless and his buddies. "Most of them fear anything different." He looked back at the alien and relaxed. "But a few of them are okay. Who are you?"

"We noticed you are the only one who is not afraid. I am Ambassador Geogram from the planet Zalma. And you are?"

"I am Private Malcolm Dow," he tilted his head with an amused smile, "from the planet Earth. You don't look like the other aliens I saw."

"No. Those are just dummies, modified clones we made to see how your people would react to beings not of your world."

Malcolm laughed. "You speak pretty good English."

"I have been monitoring your radio and television signals for decades."

"Huh." Malcolm cocked his head. "Why are you here?"

"I have come to ask for your help."

Malcolm was startled. "My help? Why me?"

"Well," Geogram paused, "you, for starters, but we need the help of your planet, and your response was better than the others. You seemed saddened when you thought the clones had died…"

Malcolm felt his stomach drop. *They saw that.*

Geogram continued, "They were never alive; they were grown in a lab, like plants."

"Yes, well… What kind of help? If you can travel through space, you must be far more advanced than us."

Geogram's purple skin turned pale and chalky, the color completely draining out of it. "Yes, we are, but my people are pacifists. We do not believe in violence, but recently, another planet, Moad, has sent ships to attack us. We do not know why they've chosen to do this, and we are trying to resolve things peacefully, but our shields will not hold for much longer. I fear if we cannot achieve peace, we will be destroyed. We have no weapons to fight."

Malcolm's jaw dropped. "So, you want *us* to fight your war for you?"

"No!" Geogram said, wide eyed. "Preferably not… We simply…wish for neutral parties for negotiation. We came here because we do not have much time. Not only is Earth the closest life-bearing planet, but we saw in your broadcasts that you recently negotiated peace. I am pleased that we have come here. And…if the worst is to come, as a failsafe, your people know how to fight. You understand?" He looked at Malcolm with a glimmer of hope in his eyes.

Idly, Malcolm noticed that the whites of Geogram's eyes were also purple. *Interesting.* He considered the ambassador's words for a moment. "I joined the army to help people, like my father did. If I were to help you, what would you want me to do?" He wasn't even sure if there was anything he *could* do.

"Will you contact your leaders for us?"

"And tell them what?" It seemed a lot to ask of a private. "Even if I could convince them, I doubt they'd send troops out into space. They'd need to know there's something in it for them."

"We are willing to share our technology with you so you can better defend your planet."

Malcolm smiled as his mind raced. He remembered his dreams of having a ray gun and flying through space. *It would be amazing!* He nodded. "Okay, wait here. I'll get Corporal Lawless... No, he would freak out. Maybe Sergeant Highton would be better, or the lieutenant."

Geogram's skin turned chalky again. "I do not believe that would be wise. They did not react well to the clones."

"What? I thought you wanted me to contact my government," Malcolm replied. "That's how we do it, through our chain of command." He shook his head, at a loss for what to do. If he couldn't go to any one of them, then what could he try? There was no way they'd let him talk to anyone higher up.

Geogram looked thoughtful. "Perhaps our information is incorrect. Do you trust them?"

Malcolm shrugged. "I don't know them very well. I'm still new to the detachment. I guess not." He shook his head in despair. "I don't know anyone here that I trust."

"We will continue our observation for now, then let you know. Here is a communicator. Call us tomorrow." Geogram tossed him a small metal object.

Malcolm fumbled catching the device but managed not to drop it into the dirt. It was a polished metal rectangle just barely smaller than a playing card but three times as thick, though still thin enough to be able to fit in his wallet. It had no buttons, no switches, no markings. It looked nothing like the clunky walkie talkies or huge radio systems that the lieutenant had. "This is a communicator? How does it work?" He looked up, but Geogram had disappeared. Malcolm glanced in every direction, including up. *Where'd he go?*

Malcolm rubbed his eyes. *Well, that was weird!* he thought. Had that just happened, or was the heat starting to get to him?

I've been out in the sun too long. He looked at the communicator in his hand. It was still there. That meant Geogram *must* have been real.

Malcolm slid the communicator into his pocket. He shook his head and stood in silence for a moment, reflecting on their entire conversation silently until it made at least a bit of sense. Then he pulled out his water flask, took a swig, and went back to work.

CHAPTER THREE

MALCOLM'S MORALS

That night, Malcolm was restless. He couldn't help but think of Geogram's request. *Technology from aliens?* He had dreamed of this since he saw his first Flash Gordon comic book. It was one of his wildest dreams, how could it be reality? *Things like this don't happen in real life.*

He rolled over again. *What if we do help them? Which humans would get their technology? What would they do with it?* Absentmindedly, his thoughts drifted back to his first year at his new school. It was laden with bullies, so to defend himself, he'd snuck a pair of brass knuckles in his pack. The first time they'd cornered him, he'd busted a few lips and gotten away. It was euphoric, and he brought them again the next day, but the bullies were expecting them. They got the brass knuckles off him, and the thing Malcolm used to protect himself was used to hurt him.

The very same thing could happen with the aliens'—Zalma's—technology. It might be next to impossible to keep it out of the wrong hands. What then?

He played every scenario over and over in his head until he was sure his brain was rotting, but still nothing came to mind. Nothing could stop the bad guys from getting it too. And if that happened, the world would just be in another shootout of mass proportions. *Maybe humanity isn't ready to handle that kind of power.*

Malcolm rolled again, and his cot squeaked. His whole body tensed, but no one else moved. If this kept up, he'd surely wake someone, so he pulled himself out of bed and shuffled into some fatigues to go for a run around the barracks. Maybe the fresh air would clear his head.

July 9, 1947

Malcolm's food was on the ground. It was a normal occurrence; Lawless was often bored at breakfast, but this time Malcolm didn't react. He got no sleep because his night's run ended shortly before the wakeup call and morning exercises. He was exhausted, half asleep, and deep in thought, staring mindlessly at the scratched surface of the table, not hearing or seeing what was happening around him.

Lawless scowled. "Aren't you going to say anything?" he demanded, then he kicked the tray so it skidded across the floor, smearing scrambled eggs, hashbrowns, and bacon in its wake.

Malcolm didn't reply and came out of his stupor just long enough to notice that his breakfast was no longer in front of him. *I must've eaten it already.* He stood and left the mess hall, falling back into his raging thoughts, leaving Lawless and his buddies dumbfounded.

"Dow! Hurry up!" the drill sergeant yelled. "What's the matter with you today? You're normally at the front of the pack!"

Malcolm skittered forward on his elbows and knees. His eyes were heavy, his limbs felt like lead weights, and his stomach seemed to have up and walked away. The earth was hot and dry under him, and even the slightest movement kicked dust up into his mouth and eyes. He propped his rifle higher to keep it out of the dirt, but it seemed to be a Herculean task, and he was only halfway through the course. Lifting his head a little more, his helmet scratched against the barbed wire. "Come on!" he mumbled to himself. He moved forward again, ignoring the pain in his elbows and knees.

Just then, an unfamiliar weight in his pocket shifted. It scraped against his leg, dragging on the ground as he moved. Malcolm froze.

The communicator. Is it moving or buzzing? Did anyone hear it? He looked around, but from what little he could see, no one was looking at him. His body was wrought with tension, and he scrambled forward a couple more feet. He couldn't check it, but if he cleared the course, maybe he could get it to stop.

He thought it buzzed again and winced as he scraped his knee on a stone.

"Dow! Pick up the pace!" the drill sergeant shouted. "You're dropping behind!"

Malcolm apologized to the sergeant as he completed the course. The man just sent him to the next exercise with a huff.

After drills, Malcolm wiped the sweat from his forehead, panting. He could fall asleep right then and there, but knew that wouldn't be appreciated by his superiors, so he resigned himself to wait until curfew.

His hand wandered down to his pocket again, the one that held the communicator. Had it been buzzing earlier or was it all in his head? He pulled it out of his pocket, staring down at the polished metal. He slipped the communicator back into his pocket.

After dinner, Malcolm hit the showers. Once again, he was lost in his thoughts—so lost, in fact, that he didn't even feel the chill of the water. As it ran across his face and down his back, he pondered the use of the tech rather than its implications.

Geogram didn't seem too scary, and he was hiding when I found him. Can he make himself invisible? Is that the technology they want to trade? Being invisible would be cool. He scrubbed away the grit from training.

As he stepped out of the showers, he saw Lawless rifling through someone else's locker. *Some people don't deserve to be invisible. He's going to blame me for that, again!* Malcolm tried reporting Lawless before, but no one believed him. *They always think that it's me because I'm black, and because Lawless usually hides something in my duffle bag. I'll have to check it later.*

Lawless turned and glared at him but said nothing.

If Malcolm was honest with himself, he wasn't even sure if *he* qualified as 'deserving' of Zalma's technology. Sure, he wanted to help people—to save people like his dad did—but what if the reason humans didn't have technology like that was because they weren't worthy of it? *Should I really be jumping into this so easily?*

Malcolm shoved that thought aside. He trusted Geogram. He wasn't sure why, but something deep within him trusted the ambassador. He'd learned a long time ago to follow his gut, his hunches, because they were usually right.

That evening, Malcolm found a quiet place at the edge of the base behind a tree, away from everyone so he could talk in private. Taking out the metal communicator, he wondered how it worked. He tapped it, then in a near whisper, said, "Hello, Ambassador?"

To his surprise, Geogram's image appeared on the metal.

"Hello, Private Dow," he greeted with a polite nod, "or do you prefer Malcolm?"

Malcolm dropped the communicator and jumped back with a yelp. He picked it up again. "Oh wow! What is this?

A television?" He frowned. "But it's way too small to be a television, and it's in color!" He was flipping it over, trying to figure out how it worked; he quickly realized that Geogram's image would switch sides every time he flipped it. He held the communicator up in the air to look at the bottom, and Geogram's image still appeared. It seemed to be tracking his face. Then he noticed that Geogram was staring at him, waiting patiently.

"Oh, hi!" Malcolm regained his composure. "Yes, umm. Are you contacting me personally or in a military role?"

"That depends. Are you still willing to help us make contact with your government?"

Malcolm had been turning their previous conversation over in his head all day, and though he could still feel a tight knot twisting in his stomach, he'd reached a decision. He couldn't see any reason for Geogram to lie to him, but that didn't change the fact that he still knew next to nothing about him or his people. The simplest way was to ask, so he did. "How do I know that I can trust you?"

Geogram replied, "Have we given you any reason not to?"

Malcolm paused for a moment. His gut was telling him that Geogram was sincere. *I'll trust him for now.* "Okay, then I guess you should stick to Private Dow."

"Excellent. We found more people who might be able to help. We sent the list to your communicator. All you have to do is ask for it."

Malcolm did, and a list was displayed in place of Geogram's image. It included very few people he knew.

"Hey, wait a minute. Where did you get this list?" When he said this, Geogram's image reappeared.

"We scanned the reactions of the people inspecting the wreckage and bodies."

"But how did you get their names?"

"The same way we are talking to you. We left communicators in the debris."

Malcolm's body tensed. "What? So, you're spying on me?"

"No!" Geogram's eyes widened, and the color drained from his light purple skin again. "This communicator is *yours*. I have already bio-coded it to respond only to your touch and voice. We cannot access it, nor can anyone else."

"*We?*" Malcolm repeated. "How many of you are here?"

"Including myself, there are six of us here on Earth."

"When do I meet the other five?"

Geogram turned to look at something—or some*one*—offscreen, then nodded. In seconds, the screen split into six sections, and the other crew members appeared. Only one other was purple like Geogram, three were different shades of green, and the last was a vivid blue.

"Greetings." Malcolm gasped, a little overwhelmed. "Okay, so if I talk to these people, what do I tell them?"

The screen went back to showing just Geogram. "The truth?" he said. He seemed perplexed by the question.

"*What?* That I met some aliens that want to talk to them? That's going to get me a straitjacket!" Malcolm's heart raced. He realized he had raised his voice and quickly turned his head to check out the surroundings, but no one was around.

"What is a straitjacket?" Geogram asked.

"Oh, never mind. I'll figure something out. How do I hang up?" As Malcolm said it, the screen went blank.

CHAPTER FOUR

THE YMIT–ZALMA'S HOPE

AAF BASECAMP, NEW MEXICO
July 10, 1947

Malcolm had another sleepless night, and again he wasn't his best during drills. He looked over the list Geogram had shown him every chance he got. *If I contact the wrong person, this whole thing could fall apart. And if I contact a bunch of different people, it's more likely something will go wrong.*

After dinner, he looked at the list again. It was organized by rank, so he figured if he went straight to the top, he'd find the highest-ranked officer Geogram thought he could trust. The name he found was one he didn't recognize: Four-Star General Frank Jones. *He must be right under the President with that kind of ranking.* The only problem now was figuring out how to get a meeting with him. *And even if I get to talk to him, what do I say?*

His eyes scanned the list again, but no other names jumped out at him. General Jones was the one he had to talk to—he could feel it. But first, he had to know exactly what he was getting into.

Malcolm called Geogram and, in a sharp tone, said, "I need to see everything."

Geogram, who already seemed surprised by the sudden call, turned pale. His mouth opened and closed a few times before he managed to form words. "What do you mean by everything? Everything in the universe? That might take some time."

"What? No! I mean everything about you and your operation. I want to meet the others in person. I want to see your tech, your war, your planet."

Wrinkles formed on Geogram's forehead. "Why?"

"Is that a problem?" Malcolm asked.

"No. I will tell you what you wish to know."

Malcolm nodded. "I can't talk where I am. Someone might hear me," he said. His eyes darted around frantically.

"Okay, walk north."

Malcolm's eyes narrowed. "How far?"

"Just walk north," Geogram repeated.

So, Malcolm walked north across the runways, passing some guards patrolling the area. The moment he was out of sight of the base, the landscape around him wobbled, shifted, and he found himself in a room, feeling a little disoriented. *Where am I?* he wondered, looking around. It was a fairly large room, and the ceiling was high and angled. Geogram was standing directly in front of him with his hands folded, and the five others that Malcolm had seen earlier were all seated at smooth silver desks, which were situated in two rows of three, like in a classroom. It reminded him almost of a station wagon if station wagons were three times bigger—and if their seats floated. *Is it magnets?* He remembered seeing people balance magnets on their opposing ends before. It almost looked the same. Behind the desks, where the windshield might be, he could see the same barren fields he was just in, so he was still on earth, on the ground. He hadn't just been beamed up, like in those alien abduction movies. *This must be their spaceship. Strange. I always thought they were round.*

"How did I get here?" Malcolm asked.

"You walked here." Geogram told him flatly. One of the others snickered behind their desk. "You might feel a little dizzy after walking through the phase variance."

"The what?" Malcolm turned around and saw the field he just came from. *Weird.* He walked out. Everything around him wobbled and shifted again, and a fresh wave of dizziness washed over him, making his stomach churn. Nonetheless, he pushed himself to turn back to the ship, only to find that it wasn't there. He stepped forward, and the ship and aliens were back in front of him. Malcolm nearly toppled over, and he grabbed one of the walls to steady himself. He was sure his face had turned green to match the three of them. He chuckled to himself.

Once he was upright again and his nausea settled, he said, "Wow, you're invisible."

One of the aliens leaned forward across her desk. She was wearing the same foil uniform as Geogram. Her bluish green skin was a drastic change from Geogram's light purple. "Yes, we are slightly out of phase. That is why you feel disoriented when you pass through the door."

"Oh." Malcolm shook his head to clear the fogginess. "What does that mean exactly?"

Geogram chuckled. "Our ship exists in another—What do you call it in your language…? universe? dimension? reality? Anyway, we no longer exist in your world, so we can't be seen or detected. Light, sound, and radar pass right through us."

"If you don't exist, then how did I get here? I mean—how did I just walk in?"

Geogram glanced at the bluish green woman for a moment, then said, "As I understand it, Joanua left the doorway partially in your reality."

Malcolm had no idea what that meant, but he knew he didn't want to go through that door again any time soon. He did his best to look professional, forcefully ignoring his lingering nausea. "Were you here the whole time?"

"No," Geogram said, "Captain Agugua set us down just a few seconds before you boarded." He nodded toward the blue man, who was sitting in the middle of the front row of desks.

"I didn't see or hear anything," Malcolm said as he tried to think back to the moment before he entered the ship the first time.

"All of our technology is built for defensive purposes. Being invisible is one of the ways we stay safe," Geogram explained with a proud smile.

"Right. What do you need me for?" Malcolm snickered slightly as a thought suddenly struck him. "You could just fly straight to the White House and meet the President."

Geogram looked at him in surprise. His complexion fluctuated for a moment, changing between green, red, and white so rapidly that he resembled a spasming Christmas display. "Do you think that would work? We can set a course now."

Okay, so sarcasm isn't something they understand. "Um, no," he said quickly, stopping the captain from setting a new course. "Doing that would probably just scare them. We have to do this carefully. We need to show them that you're friendly before we show them what you're capable of."

Geogram nodded. "I see. Then I agree." He turned his focus on the others around them. "Ah, yes. Let me introduce you to the crew. This is Captain Agugua." Geogram pointed to the captain, who rose from his seat and tipped forward into a formal bow.

"I welcome you to the bridge of the *Ymit*," he said in stiff English. "In your language, this is translated to mean *Hope*."

"Thank you," Malcolm said and returned the bow as he took another look around. *Okay, so this is just the bridge? I don't see any controls, just the desks. Are the desks the controls?*

"Our communications officer, Edugra, is sitting to the captain's right." Geogram had a warm smile as he pointed to a woman, who waved at Malcolm. "And our engineer, Joanua, is on his other side."

He smiled at them and, as dad taught him, greeted them politely. "Ladies."

Edugra and Joanua's smiles both widened. Edugra's light purple skin flushed with pink. Joanua simply nodded at Malcolm.

The last two Geogram introduced were also engineers—a married couple named Kanara and Sarara. Like Joanua, they were both bluish green. Kanara was light and clear, like the ocean, while Sarara was nearly at the other end of the spectrum; her skin was the color of ferns. Like Agugua, they both stood from their back row seats and bowed, offering murmured greetings.

For a moment, Malcolm wondered what their colors meant. Did it have something to do with their job? Before he could ask, Geogram turned to him.

"What would you like to see?"

Malcolm snapped back into his military state of mind. "Right. First, can you show me the war? I want to see what you are fighting, and what we are up against."

Malcolm's gaze followed Geogram's sweeping arm to the window as it darkened into a screen, and he saw what he assumed was the enemy ship shooting at what must be their home planet, Zalma. There were explosions, but Malcolm couldn't see what was detonating them.

"What's going on?" he asked. He saw other beams of light that bounced off something, but there wasn't anything there. "Are they hitting something invisible?"

Captain Agugua stood up again and stepped forward. As he did, his desk and chair hovered smoothly to the side. "Our deflectors bounce everything. Their bombs detect it as an impact and explode."

"Sweet." Malcolm nodded, then, just to get himself into the right frame of mind, stiffened up like he'd seen military leaders do for presentations. "Okay, I have a plan. We need to find a way to show the government that you're peaceful—that you're not trying to invade Earth or something. You also have technology we don't want our enemies to get a hold of. On Earth, any technology that one side has, the other side will develop or steal. One way or another, they will have it too, and that is too dangerous."

"What did you have in mind?" Geogram asked.

"Your invisibility might just scare them." Malcolm gave a nervous laugh. "It sure scared me."

Geogram nodded slightly, then asked in a lowered voice, "How is it that your people don't change color when you are scared?"

Malcolm's eyes widened. "You change color when you're scared?" He'd obviously noticed whenever Geogram changed color, but he'd thought it rude to ask. Was *that* the reason?

Geogram winced as he turned smoky white again. "Yes. I am afraid so. Any strong emotions trigger the change—fear, anger, excitement. We never tell lies, and we always know how each other is feeling. It is how we evolved into a pacifist society."

Malcolm nodded, though he was still staring at Geogram with a raised eyebrow. "I noticed that you keep turning white, but I didn't think it was polite to ask." He also filed that information away for later. If they changed color when they lied, he'd be able to tell if any of them were being dishonest. *Well, as long as Geogram's not lying to me now.*

Geogram ran his hands over top of each other nervously. He whispered, "I am afraid that I worry a lot. You are correct, it is quite impolite to ask. I was surprised when you didn't," he admitted. "We are new to your culture, and you are new to ours. I can speak for all of us that we will try our best to learn your social protocol. All we ask is that you do the same."

Malcolm noticed the crew members nodding. He nodded in agreement as well.

"Now, what were you saying about invisibility being scary?"

"Right." Malcolm switched back to his military voice again. "If we just flew there and then made the ship visible, they'd be afraid because they couldn't detect us. They'd wonder how long we were there and if we saw anything they didn't want us to. Then you and your ship would be immediately labeled as a threat, whether you have weapons or not. They are more likely to shoot first and ask questions later."

The crew gasped and turned white as ghosts.

"Before we show them anything you can do that is scary, we…" Malcolm thought for a moment, then corrected himself. "I'll have to earn their trust. Then I'll have to convince them that you can be trusted, that you want peace with Earth and with your enemy." He took a deep breath. "Then I have to show them how dangerous this technology can be, and if I get that far, they can meet with you."

Geogram smiled. "That sounds good. Where do we start?"

Malcolm's hands felt clammy all of a sudden. He wiped them on his fatigues. "It is not as easy as it sounds. If I can't go through the chain of command, I think I should go to the top of your list, General Jones. But, breaking the chain of command doesn't build trust, it's more likely to *break* their trust. Not to mention that I will probably have to go during the day because I don't want to risk missing him in the evening. If my detachment notices that I am missing, they'll think that I am AWOL, and I've heard that they'll arrest me on sight and throw me into the brig."

Geogram tilted his head. "What do those terms mean?"

Malcolm rolled his eyes. *How do I explain?* "Absent With Out Leave. I am leaving my assigned base to go talk to a general without permission. So, they'll want to throw me into the brig—jail. This is a big risk!" He looked up at nothing in particular. "Can you remind me, why am I doing this?"

Geogram shrugged his shoulders. "So we will give you the technology to defend your planet."

Malcolm grunted. *Is that a good enough reason?* "Getting them to trust me is hard enough. I don't know how I am going to convince them that you are peaceful. I can tell them your story, and that I have a hunch you are telling the truth, but I don't really think that will work."

There was silence in the room.

He continued, "I am sure that they would eventually realize, as I have, that with the technology to travel between stars, you could do so much damage if you wanted to. Instead, you're offering that to us. I think that should go a long way."

Malcolm saw them smiling and nodding.

"So, then I have to see if we can trust them. This invisibility is something we wouldn't want to fall into the wrong hands. Whoever had it could fly a bomb right over the White House, and they would have no idea. They need to understand that."

Geogram nodded. "You have thought this through."

Malcolm frowned. "It comes from experience, from people blaming me for things I didn't do, just because of how I look." The ship's crew all turned more bluish as empathetic expressions crossed their faces, and Geogram was about to speak, but Malcolm interrupted before he could.

"Can you show me something else?"

For a moment, it almost seemed like Geogram wasn't going to let him steer the conversation away, but then he asked, "Would you like a tour of our ship?"

Malcolm hummed. "No, actually," he said. "I think if I see anything more, my brain is going to explode."

Geogram's eyes went so wide Malcolm was afraid they'd burst from his head, and he quickly mumbled how that would be "most distressing."

"That's just a figure of speech. I didn't get much sleep last night, and all of this is too much to take in." He sort of wanted a tour, but he didn't have the energy to see more. He knew the ship had to be bigger than the bridge, obviously. Geogram had told him that they'd traveled five months to get to earth. That was a long time to stay in a room with five other people.

Malcolm sat down on a floating chair, offered by Edugra. He was too tired to ask how it worked, especially after the door explanation, he knew he wouldn't understand. When he thanked her, her face flushed pink again. *Is she blushing?* Malcolm wondered. He almost laughed. *Some things are universal, I guess.*

He watched a few more angles of war footage on the big screen up front, though he probably only saw half of it as he cycled through the new information in his head. A pacifist alien race attacked by another planet. Malcolm couldn't count all the times he'd wondered what would happen if Martians invaded Earth when he was a child. *Do Martians even exist? Would they have technology like this?* The people of Zalma—Zalmen, or whatever they were called—had all sorts of defense technology, but...

"What about weapons?" he asked, turning to Captain Agugua.

Agugua turned the same smoky white that Geogram became when he was nervous, though it was much more jarring considering how bright the captain usually was. "We are pacifists," he enunciated clearly once his skin returned to normal. "We don't have anything that resembles what you would call a weapon."

Malcolm frowned. He glanced back at the screen, which showed off the same enemy ship shooting more beams of light at the Zalmen's planetary shields. "Nothing? No ray guns?" When Agugua shook his head, Malcolm felt his heart sink. He'd always dreamed of having a ray gun.

Joanua rose from her desk and joined them. "We use lasers for scientific research, medical procedures, and as a tool for cutting," she offered. "I'm sure they could be repurposed, but only if our scientists had assistance from your government's experts. I'm afraid our people would not know the first thing about weaponizing our technology on their own."

Malcolm raised his eyebrows. "Okay, but you seriously have nothing that's already a weapon?" he asked incredulously.

Edugra moved to the edge of her seat, and it hovered closer to them. "We are a peaceful people. We wouldn't know what to do with a weapon if we had it."

Malcolm shook his head again. "Well, it looks like the scariest thing you have is your invisible, silent ship. Darn," he chuckled, "I can't tell you how much I wanted a ray gun." He looked down and was in deep thought. Suddenly, he perked up. "Wait! I remember that Geogram was invisible when we first met. Is that something you can do, or can you make *me* invisible?"

"You would have to wear one of our suits," Agugua said.

Malcolm eyed Agugua's glossy foil suit and laughed softly. "They're never going to let me in to see a general in one of those silver outfits," he said. "Couldn't you just make it so that *my* uniform could make me invisible? By putting that invisibility tech into my clothes or something?"

Joanua regarded him for a moment thoughtfully. "I hadn't thought of that before, but I suppose it could work," she said.

Malcolm beamed. He hadn't expected it to *actually* be possible. "Should I go get a spare uniform for you?"

"No, no. I can scan your clothing now. Stand up, please." She stepped forward, pulling a small device out of her pocket. It looked the same as Malcolm's communicator.

"Anything else you need, Private?" Agugua asked as she finished scanning him.

Malcolm watched Joanua disappear through one of the side doors. "How would I turn it on?" he asked.

"Voice commands. The uniform would be connected to your communicator, so all you would have to do is say *communicator, activate cloak*." Agugua suddenly vanished. Malcolm heard a sigh. "I hate it when that happens… Communicator, deactivate cloak." The air shimmered where he had been standing, and he reappeared.

Malcolm snapped his fingers. He'd been meaning to ask how his communicator worked. Now was his chance. "So I don't actually have to be holding my communicator to activate it?"

Edugra's chair wobbled in midair for a moment as she said, "You can hold your communicator, or you can say its name. If you don't, it won't respond." She giggled. "That's a good thing, too, or it would be trying to do everything we say."

"Can I give it a different name?" Malcolm asked.

"You can give it a different name if you want," Edugra replied. "My communicator's name is E."

Malcolm grinned excitedly. "What else can it do?"

"What else do you want it to do?" Geogram asked.

"Uhhh…" Malcolm thought for a few seconds, then said, "I'll get back to you on that."

It was then that Joanua returned from the other room. In her arms was an exact copy of the army fatigues that Malcolm was wearing. "Your uniform is ready," she said, handing it to him. "I've installed nanites into the fabric. They should connect to your communicator as soon as you put it on."

Malcolm stared at it. He ran his fingers over the fabric, marveling at how soft it was. *How can there be technology in this?* He thought it would have to be crinkly and metallic—like the crew's uniforms, but the outfit was exactly like his own! "Wow! That was fast. Thank you." He turned to Geogram. "I was thinking that we should go directly to General Jones. Any idea where I can find him?"

"He has an office in a building nearby. It is where they are keeping our decoy ship's debris," Agugua replied.

Malcolm nodded. But how would he get there? He grinned again. *I may as well take advantage of their spacecraft. I am helping them, after all.* "Can you take me there tomorrow when he arrives?"

"Yes, of course. We will notify you on your communicator," Agugua said.

"What? With a beep or something?" Malcolm remembered feeling his blood pressure rising when he thought his pocket was making weird noises in the middle of morning drills. He did *not* want to go through that again.

"You can set it to do that if you like, but by default, it is set to vibrate for notifications," Edugra said.

"Vibration?" Malcolm breathed a sigh of relief. "So, no one will know besides me?"

"Correct."

"Man!" Malcolm felt a rush of adrenalin. "You guys make great spy equipment."

Agugua turned a vibrant red, then yellow, then back to red. "Our equipment is for defense," he said insistently, voice a little higher than usual. "We are *not* spies!"

"And yet you have spy equipment hidden in the debris?" Malcolm reminded them. He gave the captain a good-natured smile, hoping to calm him down. He hadn't meant to offend him.

That only seemed to make it worse.

Agugua's skin returned to yellow and stayed that way, though aside from the shift of hue, he made no other move. "We are protecting what is ours." He sniffed pointedly.

"Fair enough." *Yellow must mean angry.* "I'm sorry. I meant it as a compliment."

Agugua returned to his normal vibrancy. He looked down; his mouth was pinched in shame. "No, I am the one who is sorry."

Malcolm held out his hand for the captain to shake before he even thought that it might not be something the Zalmen did. To his relief, Agugua knew what to do, and clasped his hand in a firm shake. Malcolm turned to the door. The desert field was still there in front of him, unchanged. The moment he saw it, his stomach rolled over as he remembered how sick he felt when he entered the ship before. He *really* didn't want to go through that again, but the only other option was staying on the ship forever, and he couldn't do that, unfortunately.

He waved to the crew and said, "I'll wait for your signal tomorrow, then I will meet you here." Then he took a deep breath, held it, and stepped out onto the dirt.

CHAPTER FIVE

NOW YOU SEE ME...

A A F   B A S E C A M P ,   N E W   M E X I C O
July 10, 1947

M alcolm was really excited to try out his new toy. He went straight to his barracks and changed into his new uniform, then checked that no one was around and said, "Communicator, make me invisible."

No, those aren't the words. He looked down and saw that he didn't have a shadow, though he could still see himself, so he walked to a window. There was no reflection staring back at him. *Yes! I guess it knew what I meant.* He looked around, grinning. *I wonder where Lawless is.* It wasn't like he cared about what the other soldier was doing, but he was always so hostile; Malcolm wondered what Lawless was like when he wasn't around.

Malcolm tried to walk without making any noise. It took a few tries before he realized that people couldn't hear him. *Maybe it's because I'm 'out of phase'?* He tried to remember what Joanua had told him. *This will be hard to get used to.*

He walked around until he saw Lawless talking with some of the other soldiers on the outer edge of the base in the shade of a tall tree. All of them seemed to be his buddies; they were laughing and joking around. Malcolm already knew that they did that. Bored, Malcolm was just about to leave, but then he saw Sergeant Highton approaching.

Highton sneered at Lawless. "I heard you had a few pathetic performances with Dow lately. Are you losing your touch?" he mocked.

Lawless stepped away from his buddies to look Highton in the eye. "What's your problem?" he sneered back, puffing his chest.

"You let that upstart put you in your place."

"He did *not!*" Lawless shouted. He was slightly shorter than Highton, but he still managed to get in the sergeant's face before he turned and stalked away.

Highton scoffed, then looked over Lawless's gaggle of friends. "Why do you even bother following this loser around?"

"Because of his family," Private Martin said with a shrug. "If you want to get anywhere in this army, you need his connections."

Highton waved his hand dismissively. "His family probably thinks he's as useless as I do."

"That's not true!" Lawless spun around again, glaring at Highton. "You better apologize, or you'll...you'll...you'll regret it," said Lawless.

"Knucklehead." Highton rolled his eyes. "You can't even put a boy like *Dow* in his proper place. What makes you think you can do anything against me? Your father must be so *proud.*" His lip curled into a vicious grin as he stared down at Lawless.

For once, Lawless looked small.

Malcolm was so shocked that he almost forgot they couldn't see him; that he was just a fly on the wall. He couldn't believe what he was hearing. *Is this how it always is?* he wondered. How had he not seen it?

Oh, right, because when I'm around, I'm the butt of the joke. Even so, he'd never thought that Lawless, of all people, would be a victim of bullying. Malcolm knew that Lawless's family was full of high-ranking officers, after all. He was a corporal, but Malcolm never expected it to take long before Lawless was promoted again. Now, he wasn't so sure.

Highton threw back his head and laughed. "Let's get out of here." He spat in the dirt at Lawless's feet, then walked away. With one glance thrown over his shoulder, he had the others following him, leaving Lawless on his own by the tree.

Malcolm was about to step aside before an idea bloomed in his head, and he instead stuck out his leg. Highton tripped. He hit the ground hard, face smacking a rock. Seconds later, he was back on his feet, a massive red welt on his forehead and sand still stuck to his sweaty skin. His eyes shot to each of the men around him accusingly, but he didn't say a word.

Everyone around him burst into laughter, Lawless and Malcolm included. Highton grunted, wiped his face off and stomped away. The others clambered after him, leaving Lawless and Malcolm together—not that anyone knew Malcolm was there.

Malcolm contemplated Lawless curiously. His former enemy seemed so beat down, nothing like the evil adversary Malcolm had built up in his head. What happened next surprised him more than anything.

Lawless was holding back tears. As soon as he thought he was alone, he dropped down on the roots of the tree, head in his hands. His shoulders were shaking.

Malcolm didn't know what to do. Was he intruding on a private moment? Should he leave? He knew that his presence wouldn't be welcome, but for some reason, his gut was telling him not to leave Lawless alone. He sat next to Lawless, not close enough to touch; he didn't want to blow his cover.

"I'm so sorry, dad," Lawless whispered, voice trembling. "I'm trying. I'm trying, I swear. I'm just doing what you taught me to do. You—you always said I had to stand tall, be confident. I had to prove that I was better than the other guy." He dug his hands into his hair and sniffled, then he wiped furiously at his nose. "Why don't they respect me like they do you? I am trying to make you proud. I just *don't* understand what I'm doing wrong."

Malcolm felt sorry for Lawless. Then he felt angry at *himself* for feeling sorry for Lawless. This was the man who harassed him daily just because he was black; why should he care? But for some reason, he did.

Maybe…maybe it wouldn't hurt to help Lawless out—maybe then he wouldn't feel so inclined to take his anger out on others. "Communicator," he muttered, "I want him to hear me." A strange tingling sensation washed over him, and he figured that it worked. Malcolm spoke in a soft, ghostly manner, as he walked away from Lawless to throw his voice. "Squeeze the trigger, don't pull. That's how you hit the targets."

Funny. Lawless said he'd figure out how I 'cheated' during target practice, and then I end up telling him myself. Half of him hoped that Lawless didn't hear, but the other half was curious what he would think if he did.

His struggle is different from mine, Malcolm thought as he turned over this new information in his head. *He has friends, but they're not real. He has a dad, but he isn't loved. We're as different as can be, but we are both bullied.*

When he got back to the barracks, Malcolm looked around to make sure nobody was within sight, then said, "Communicator, make me visible."

CHAPTER SIX

MISSION ZERO

AAF BASECAMP, NEW MEXICO
July 11, 1947

Malcolm was eating breakfast when his communicator vibrated, and he knew that meant the general was in his office. He swallowed what food he could, grabbed his toast, and headed for the rendezvous point.

Sweat dripped down from his forehead. He hoped that no one would notice and report that he was missing during training exercises, but he also knew that this was unlikely. At first, they would probably just send one person to check his barracks and such. If he was able to get back before afternoon training, he might just have to do extra laps or something. Any later in the day, and he would probably be sent to the brig for up to a month.

ZALMA OUTREACH VESSEL–YMIT

The journey was surreal. Looking out the window, Malcolm saw the landscape moving in a blur around them, but it felt like they were standing still. Never mind the fact that he'd barely sat down before they stopped in front of an old warehouse. "How far away are we?" he asked.

"We are approximately ten miles from your base," Captain Agugua said.

MALCOLM DOW: EPISODE 1

Malcolm swallowed thickly. "Ten miles? How? It's only been about a minute! And I didn't feel a thing! How is that possible?"

"Our ship has its own gravity. You wouldn't feel the effects of anything outside," Joanua said, looking smug.

"Really? Wow!" Malcolm looked at the screen and saw the building with silhouettes of people overlapping it. Most of the people had names beside them. "You can see the people inside?"

"Yes. The screen is displaying a visual image of the building with their body heat signatures overlapped, as well as other data. You can see General Jones is in the office at the far right of the building."

The view on screen then rotated so that they could see the floor plan of the building. Jones's office was in the right rear corner. In the middle was a large space with the decoy ship's debris, and on the left were rows of racks and a variety of rooms such as the kitchen, mess hall, and a room with a reinforced wall. *That must be the brig.*

"Great! Can you drop me off behind the tree closest to the entrance?"

Agugua tapped his desk a few times, and the ship touched down gently.

"Thank you." As Malcolm exited the ship, his heart began racing. His hands felt clammy again. *I'm a private going to see a general. They're never going to let me see him. I wish I could use the invisibility, but if I suddenly appear, they are likely to label me a threat and shoot first. I have to stick to the plan.*

Flashbacks of the beatings he'd suffered at the hands of his fellow soldiers nagged him. His pace slowed, and he wondered if he should run while he still could. The guard station was only a few hundred feet away, but it felt like the packed dirt was stretching out further and further in front of him. An idea popped into his head—they might let a courier in.

Malcolm saluted the guards on duty. "Private Dow reporting with an urgent message for General Jones." He tried to look as confident as possible.

One of the guards flipped through his records. "You're not on the list," he said.

"It's an urgent message. Top Secret. They didn't want to risk anyone intercepting." Malcolm felt his heart race. *Well, it's the truth!*

The other guard was looking down at Malcolm. His cold blue eyes seemed to be taking him apart. "How did you get here?"

"My Jeep broke down. I had to walk the rest of the way, sir!"

The guards whispered to each other for a moment, then the first one pushed Malcolm toward an entrance to the left. "Let's go!" The guard was walking close behind with his rifle across his chest, ready for action.

Malcolm knew that Jones was on the right, and he doubted that he was being led to the mess hall. They must've been taking him to the brig, and he had a hunch that once he was locked up, he wouldn't see Jones. He had to quickly come up with a plan. The hot desert sun was already getting in his eyes. *That's it!* A few steps before the entrance Malcolm closed his eyes momentarily to adjust to the dark. As they entered the building, Malcolm spun around and punched the guard in the face, sending him sprawling on the ground. Malcolm ran to the racks, and he looked back to see the guard squinting, trying to focus. *It worked! His eyes are still trying to adjust!*

He tried to remember the floor plan. Jones was at the back of the far right, and he was near the front of the far left. He would have to cross the warehouse somehow, but the middle was filled with scientists looking at the debris.

As Malcolm shifted between the racks, he wondered why the alarm didn't go off. He could hear the guard running behind him and switched to a different row. He grabbed the communicator from his pocket and whispered, "Make me invisible," but as he said it, he heard the guard behind him.

"Halt!" the guard said as he ran toward Malcolm.

For some reason, the guard could still see him, so Malcolm ran behind another row, then hid between the pallets.

The guard was close behind, but as he turned down Malcolm's row, he stopped. Walking slowly and quietly, the guard looked through the pallets. Malcolm was sure the guard could see his toes sticking out, but as the guard came close his facial expression stayed the same, and he walked right past.

Malcolm looked for his shadow but didn't see it. He was invisible, but why didn't it work earlier, when he first said the command? He remembered that no one could hear him when he was invisible. He wondered if the communicator could talk. "Communicator?"

"How may I help?" came the reply.

I wasn't really expecting a reply. "Why didn't I go invisible when I requested it?"

"I am programmed to prevent outsiders from seeing you transition. I had to wait until he couldn't see you."

"That's smart, but I wish I knew that before." Malcolm waited for a reply, but the communicator was silent.

Malcolm sat down. Since he was invisible, he was in no rush. "Communicator, Edugra said I could change your name if I wanted."

"Yes. My default name is Communicator. What would you like to call me?"

Malcolm leaned his head back against the racks, trying to think of a name. He thought of his comic book hero names, Flash, Gordon, Buck, Rogers, Superman, and Batman just didn't seem right. He remembered his cousin Benny talking about his dream of writing comic books about a black space captain on a ship called Federation Nineteen. What was the captain's name...? He jolted up suddenly. "Benjamin; can I call you Benjamin?"

"Yes, you can call me Benjamin."

"It's nice to meet you, Benjamin."

"It is nice to meet you too, Malcolm," Benjamin said.

CHAPTER SEVEN

THE GENERAL

AAF WAREHOUSE, NEW MEXICO
July 10, 1947

Malcolm exited the racks and casually walked through the middle of the warehouse knowing that no one could see him. Some of the scientists were looking at the foil they collected with microscopes, and others were dipping the foil in different liquids.

Malcolm sprinted across to the back right of the building, to where Jones's office was. Just as he reached the door, the two guards came from behind him.

One of them put his ear to the general's door. "No, he's not talking. He must still be alone," he whispered.

"Good," whispered the other.

"If we don't find the intruder, General Scornson will have our hides."

They ran right past Malcolm, then he heard the outside door close. The moment they were gone, he let out an ecstatic laugh. *So that's why they didn't sound the alarm. They are spies for another general.*

"Benjamin, if they return, please let me know. I don't want them to eavesdrop on our conversation."

"Certainly."

Malcolm looked at the door marked 'General Jones'. He

reached up to knock but didn't see his shadow. "Benjamin, make me visible."

"Done."

He knocked.

A voice came from within the office. "Enter."

The door creaked as he opened it. He closed it behind him and stepped toward the general, who was sitting behind his desk. What was left of his hair was shot through with gray, but despite his age, he still maintained a bulk of muscle around his shoulders and down his arms.

Malcolm saluted sharply. "General Jones, sir?"

The general put down his pen and set aside what he was writing. "Yes, and you are?"

"Private Malcolm Dow, sir."

Jones leaned back in his chair. "Well, Private Dow, how did you get in here?"

"I walked, but then the guards didn't want me to see you, sir, so I had to force my way in."

"Really? What is so urgent?"

"Aliens, sir," Malcolm said, surprising even himself with his directness.

Jones stared at him silently for a moment, his face not giving away his thoughts. Then he stood, rounded his desk, and stepped forward until he was nose-to-nose with Malcolm. "Aliens?" he asked softly, his mouth barely moving. "What about them?"

Malcolm didn't budge, looking straight forward like he was trained to do. "Are they friendly, sir?" he asked.

The general stepped back with a heavy sigh. "I hope so," he said, then he chuckled. "Otherwise, we could be in a lot of trouble, don't you think?"

"Yes, sir."

"Have you met them?"

"Yes, sir." The words just came out of Malcolm's mouth, surprising him.

Jones nodded. "At ease." He returned to his desk and sat down. "This morning I had a hunch that someone would come to introduce me to them today."

"A hunch, sir?" Malcolm repeated, not sure if he heard correctly.

"Yes, a hunch."

Malcolm had his own hunch that he could trust Jones.

"Where are you stationed? Are they expecting you? We don't want them to think you are AWOL, do we?"

"Roswell, sir. Yes, sir. Thank you, sir."

Jones called Malcolm's base and told them that Private Dow was on special assignment. "Now that we have dealt with that, tell me about the aliens." Jones motioned for Malcolm to sit down as well.

Malcolm took the chair opposite. "They are pacifists, sir."

"Yes, with advanced technology." Jones paused. "The kind we wouldn't want our enemies to have, correct?"

"How did you know, sir?"

Jones smirked. "I'm a Four-Star General, aren't I?" he asked, his eyes twinkling. He tapped his temple. "I know things. Now, what are they willing to give us in exchange for our help?"

"Wait a minute." Malcolm was sweating again. He wiped one of his sleeves across his forehead. After a few seconds, he dropped his hands and looked at Jones. "You mean to tell me that I was sweating this whole time, trying to figure out how I was going to tell you, and you knew? How?"

"I was in Washington with the President the other day, and he told me—" Jones changed his voice to indicate he was repeating the President. "*Something, or should I say some*one, *crash-landed in Roswell, New Mexico yesterday.*" He smirked, amused by his own impression. "He told me he needed my 'unbiased gut instincts,' my 'hunches,' and my 'Sherlock Holmes-like deductive powers.' That's how I knew this was something serious."

Malcolm's fingers dug into the fabric along his thighs. "But how did you...?"

"Be patient," Jones said. "The President told me they found what they thought was an airdrop container. Inside were three non-human bodies. Am I correct in assuming that you were the one to find these bodies?"

Malcolm nodded. "Yes, I looked inside and reported it to my lieutenant. Those were just dummies, though. When I went to pick up debris far away from the initial crash site, I met them for real."

"Dummies, hm? *Interesting.*" Jones nodded. "That would explain why the autopsy revealed no obvious cause of death. The doctor just guessed that they'd suffocated, but he didn't have any healthy bodies to compare them to." Jones stood and started pacing back and forth behind the desk.

Malcolm's eyes followed the movement.

"Initially," the general began, "I thought that they were children, but then I learned that the crash was only about a hundred miles east of the nuclear test site. The debris from the crash indicates that it flew over the test site before it landed. That was suspicious. If it was a simple ship, a lifeboat, why would they put dead children inside? Unless," he raised a finger sharply in the air, "it was a decoy."

Malcolm leaned closer, intrigued.

"I thought it might be a hoax, but that didn't make sense either. A decoy made the most sense, but what were they trying to distract us from? Could another country be trying to steal our nuclear plans from the test site while we investigated the crash?" Jones sat down again. "No, because we increased security when we heard of the crash, and they must have assumed we would."

Malcolm nodded, but he didn't speak; Jones was on a roll.

"So, I thought that if it's aliens, they have technology advanced enough to travel between planets, so why would they be interested in our nuclear bombs? Surely, they could make their own. Perhaps, if they crashed, they would need a powerful energy source for their ship, but then we'd find a larger ship, not just a lifeboat. Either the main ship didn't land, or it's still here somewhere. And if it *didn't* land, it's not a problem—*yet!* If it's here, where is it, and what's it doing?" Jones stood up and started pacing again, full of nervous energy. "I tried to imagine myself as a space alien and ran several scenarios in my head. I imagined that if we could destroy a city with one bomb, they could have destroyed *us* if they wanted to. And since they did not contact us, I assumed they must be unable to. Or," he paused again, thinking. "Or they are being cautious, maybe they are manipulating us.

"Then, I had a hunch that the aliens were afraid and friendly," Jones sat down and reached across his desk holding up his hand in a fist. "I always trust my hunches, as does the President. They've never steered me wrong before. From there, I figured that the ship must be a decoy, a test, and the aliens must be watching us to see our reactions. If they were simply afraid, they wouldn't risk sending a decoy in the first place because it reveals their presence here. Therefore, they want something from us—something they can't get without us."

Jones paused again, and Malcolm thought he was done, but before he could get a word in, Jones kept talking.

"What could they want? Why the nuclear test site? Weapons? No, they should have more advanced weapons than us. Or they could've just stolen them."

Malcolm broke out in laughter.

Jones grunted. "I take it that's a *no.*"

Malcolm calmed himself down. "Sorry, sir. Yes, that's a *no.* They do have advanced technology and tools that can be converted into weapons, but no weapons ready to go. Shame, too," he sighed, "I really wanted a ray gun."

Jones chuckled. "I couldn't figure it out. I thought it was our weapons they wanted, but why not just take them? Were they afraid of us, even though we have less technology? Then it became obvious to me. It's not our weapons they want, but our people—people who know how to fight. They want our *help.* Perhaps they are under siege, but they were unsure of how we would take them, being from another planet, so they sent a decoy, and watched."

Malcolm was thoroughly impressed. He wasn't sure whether he should clap or not. He did anyway, just to be safe. "You are half right. They want us and our weapons as a backup plan, but it is our negotiators they are primarily interested in."

Jones raised his eyebrows. "Really... Anyway, on the off chance that I was wrong, I was planning to build a defense strategy."

Malcolm raised his eyebrows.

"Well, I would've, but then I realized that if they were watching us and saw that we were preparing to attack them, we could start a war before we had a chance to talk. I was thinking of the speed needed to travel between planets and imagined being able to fly and drop a bomb anywhere in the world in less than a second. Us having that capability is scary enough to think about, but what if our enemies got hold of it? I predicted that the world would fall to ruin in less than six months."

"I had the same concern," Malcolm said. "I spent a few sleepless nights thinking about it."

Jones nodded. "I also had to consider their enemy. If *our* aliens could not face it… What if their enemy came here?"

Malcolm paled. "Yeah, that's a scary thought. I hadn't thought about that."

"Indeed, so I told the President that we must ally ourselves with these aliens. If they seek our help, we must help them, and in return, ask for their technology to allow us to defend ourselves and our planet. I also told him that if we *did* gain the aliens' technology, we couldn't keep it on Earth. Someone might steal it."

"And what did he say?"

Jones grunted again, hiding a laugh. "He wasn't impressed. I suspect he was more concerned with what the public would think if they found out he was dealing with aliens."

"Yes," Malcolm agreed, "there is enough division between people already. Between blacks and whites. You don't seem to be bothered by it, though. Why?"

Jones huffed. "I don't understand it. We are all people, blacks and whites, are we not? I've lived enough to know that it's not a person's appearance that's important, it's their actions."

At the general's words, Malcolm felt a lead weight drop into his stomach. Sure, the general wasn't a person to judge on appearance, but how could he understand Malcolm's plight?

Neither could Malcolm understand how Geogram felt. Malcolm didn't know what it would feel like to have weapons shot at Earth. He wanted to help Geogram, but he could never understand.

Neither was the general acknowledging all that had been done between their races. He was speaking like the divide didn't exist. He didn't see it.

Before Malcolm could speak, the general continued.

"No. Instead, I asked the President whether he would rather deal with these aliens or with their enemies. That got his attention, and he reluctantly agreed to ally with them and put me in charge of this 'Top Secret' project." Jones's face was set with a serious expression.

"Yes sir, I understand."

Jones relaxed. "Good. Now when am I going to meet these aliens?"

Malcolm pulled out the communicator. "Connect us to Ambassador Geogram." When Geogram's face appeared on the screen, Malcolm said, "General Jones already had it all figured out."

Geogram nodded, though he looked quite surprised. "Stimulating," he said. "Let me speak to him, please."

"Interesting!" Jones exclaimed as he received the communicator. He took a moment to admire the device before speaking. "General Frank Jones here. I understand that you are the ambassador for your people?"

Geogram's image was displayed on both sides of the device so both humans could see him. He nodded politely to the general. "Yes. Ambassador Geogram, at your service."

Jones grinned at him. "I can appreciate the precautions you took to protect yourselves. I can get you the help you need to defend your planet and negotiate if your people will supply us with the technology to defend ours. I think we can help each other, don't you?"

"Indeed, we are hoping to negotiate peace with our invaders, the people of Moad. What has Private Dow shared with you so far?"

"He hasn't shared much. I'm a military strategist, so I figured it out on my own. He just confirmed my suspicions. I do have one question left unanswered, though. How did you know that you could trust Private Dow and myself?"

"Our technology can detect such things as lying, fear, and hatred."

"Interesting," Jones said. "I have already spoken with our President about helping you, and I have compiled a list of possible recruits for you and Corporal Dow to check out."

"Corporal Dow?" Malcolm was wide-eyed. *That's not my rank; he knows that. What is he doing?* He stood up from his seat. "Um, the guards here are probably not safe. I overheard them talking about a General Scornson, sir."

Jones raised a single gray eyebrow in Malcolm's direction. "Oh, really? They will be transferred out immediately." He smiled. "And I am transferring you to my command. Initially you will have to say that you are my assistant, but the truth is that you are in charge of recruitment."

"Thank you, sir, but you do realize that I'm black, sir?" *That was a stupid thing to say! Why did I just say that?*

"Exactly! And anyone who won't accept you is certainly not going to accept aliens. You can eliminate anyone who reacts negatively to you before you even open your mouth. If they pass that test, you ask them the same thing you asked me, if they think aliens are friendly. If they pass that test as well, you tell them to report to me for a top-secret mission, which is the truth."

"Yes, sir..." Malcolm sat back down. *Is this really happening?* He was pretty sure this was a dream, but he didn't dare try to wake up if it was.

The general turned back to the communicator. "Ambassador—I think it's high time we met face to face."

DID YOU ENJOY THIS BOOK?

Your feedback helps me provide the best quality books and helps other readers like you discover them.

It would mean the world to me if you took two minutes to share your thoughts about this book. You can leave a review with the retailer of your choice and/or send an email to *tony@tonybrichard.com* with your honest feedback.

Thank you, I really appreciate it.

ACKNOWLEDGMENTS

Thank you to everyone who has helped this book become a reality. To my wife, Lydia, without whom this wouldn't be possible, to my Beta readers, to Alex Perkins for designing the beautiful cover, to Carolin Petersen for editing and adding all of the final touches, and to every person who pitched in their ideas and opinions.

A special thanks to Gene Roddenberry, George Lucas, Dean Devlin, Roland Emmerich, Brad Wright, Jonathan Glassner, Ronald D. Moore, Ben Nedivi, Matt Wolpert, Greg Berlanti, and Todd Helbing for their wonderful creations (Star Trek, Star Wars, Stargate, For All Mankind, and Superman and Lois) that have and continue to inspire me.

PRONUNCIATION GUIDE

Ymit	YEM—it
Geogram	Ge—OG—ram
Agugua	A—GU—gwa
Joanua	Jo—ANN—wa
Edugra	Ed—OOO—gra
Sarara	Sa—RARE—ah
Kanara	Can—AR—ah
Zalma	ZALL—mah
Zalmen	ZALL—men
Moad	Moe—ADD
Moadites	Moe—ADD—eytes

OTHER WORKS COMING SOON!

NEGOTIATIONS
Ryan Wilcox: Episode 1

THREE GENERALS:
THE GOOD, THE BAD, AND THE UNDECIDED
Greg Newman: Episode 1

I DON'T WANT TO BUILD BOMBS
Mary Goss: Episode 1

ABOUT THE AUTHOR

Tony B. Richard lives in Langley, British Columbia. He is a computer programmer (coder) and instructor. This grand adventure has been in his head for decades, and during the Covid-19 pandemic, he thought it was finally time to put it down on paper.

"Differences are something to be celebrated, not feared."
—TONY B. RICHARD

YOU CAN CONTACT HIM WITH QUESTIONS OR COMMENTS AT:

Website: www.tonybrichard.com
Email: tony@tonybrichard.com

Facebook: EarthsSecretAlliance
Twitter: @TonyBRichard1
Instagram: tony_b_richard
Goodreads: Tony B. Richard

Printed in Great Britain
by Amazon